A TRIP TO REMEMBER

[signature]

To: Mrs. Ryan's Class —

Thank a veteran!

&

Michele [signature]

A TRIP TO REMEMBER

Written by
MICHELE SPRY
Illustrated by Peggy A. Guest

SPRY Publishing
7301 W. Henderson Road
Columbia, MO 65202
www.MicheleSpry.com

Photographs on pages 125-128, and 130 by Lollipop Photography

ISBN 13: 978-0-9887782-8-3 - hardcover with jacket
ISBN 13: 978-0-9887782-7-6 - epub
Library of Congress Control Number: 2016910064

Lt. Col. Ferrill A. Purdy

THIS BOOK IS DEDICATED TO
LT. COL. FERRILL A. PURDY

Thank you for your service to our country, your friendship but most of all, allowing me the opportunity to listen and share your story.

★ ★ ★

To the men and women who have served and are currently serving our country,

I just wanted to take a moment to say thank you for the sacrifices you have made not only for our country but in your own lives. You stepped forward putting your own lives on the line every day to protect our country and our freedom. While many of you would simply say that you were just doing your job, I want you to know that you are always appreciated and never taken for granted.

Thank you for your service.

Love, A Grateful American

CHAPTER ONE

Tomorrow was the last day of 4th grade.

"Jax, let's go buddy. It's time to eat breakfast." said Jaxon's mom. "You don't want to be late for your second-to-last day of school!"

Jaxon made his way to the kitchen still sleepy and yawning. He gave a quick comb of his hair with his fingers and sat down to eat his bowl of cereal with his little sister.

"Bubby eat!" said Abbygail, Jaxon's sister as she gave him a quick smile and a little giggle.

Jaxon's dad, Grant, was loading up his work trailer with materials and tools for the day. "Jaxon we have about 5 minutes until we need to get going so I can get you to school on time and make it over to the job site."

"Alright, dad," said Jaxon.

"Bye, bye." said Abbygail as she gave a big wave.

"You are so silly Abby!" grinned Jaxon as he looked at his sister. Jaxon took his bowl over to the sink and rinsed it out before placing it in the dishwasher. Just then Jaxon's mom came into the room.

"Thanks Jax! Now don't forget to brush your teeth and your hair, *for real*, before heading off to school." Jaxon gave a nod and headed to his room.

"Bubby go bye-bye?" asked Abbygail.

"Yes sweet baby girl, Bubby is going to school," said Jaxon's mom as she smiled.

CHAPTER TWO

Hooonk, Hooonk!

"Jaxon! Come on buddy - we're going to be late for your baseball game!" called Jaxon's dad, Grant. Jaxon quickly said goodbye to his buddies on the playground and ran over to the truck.

"Hey dad! Sorry to keep you waiting. My team was winning the foursquare game today!" Jaxon said as he was catching his breath.

"That's great! Buckle your seat belt; we'll get you over to Community Fields just in time for warm up," Jaxon's dad said.

After Jaxon buckled up, he asked, "So, how was your day, dad?"

"Well it was pretty good! We are almost done with the house over on Waymore Street for Mr. & Mrs. Percy and started a little remodel project for Ms. Baker. You remember Ms. Baker, don't you?" said Jaxon's dad.

"Is she the older lady that we helped build a wheelchair ramp for last summer?" asked Jaxon.

"Exactly! She asked how you were doing!" Just then they pulled into the ball fields. Jaxon grabbed his uniform, shoes and bat and headed for the field. "See you in a few minutes, dad!" yelled Jaxon.

Jaxon's ball team, The Stingers, played against the Cobras - who were really good. The Stingers lost this game 2-0. Several members of the team were mad and frustrated because they didn't win. One of the team members, Cash, began to blame another team member, Carter, because he didn't hit the ball in the 9th inning that would have tied the game as the bases were loaded. Jaxon saw how much this bothered Carter and told him he did a good job and this game wasn't meant to be won by them.

"Hang in there Carter, we'll get them next time. It wasn't your fault and you did your best," Jaxon said as he gave Carter a high five and a smile. "See you tomorrow at school!"

CHAPTER THREE

And today was the LAST day of 4th grade.

As they pulled up to Eagle Ridge Elementary School, Jaxon saw his buddies waiting outside for him. He reached over and gave his dad a fistbump, and told him to have a great day and he would see him after school. Jaxon was excited to see his friends. They would finally be 5th graders by the end of the day and this was a moment they have all waited for since kindergarten.

In the classroom they were greeted by Mrs. Sappington, their 4th grade teacher. Throughout the morning they spent time with their classmates and reflected on the year they had. Mrs. Sappington even told them how proud she was of them for being such awesome students this year.

Since it was the last day of school they just had a few little things to finish up. The students were busy emptying out their desks, cleaning up their classroom, along with a little joshing around. When the bell rang, everyone grabbed their lunches or lunch money and headed to the cafeteria. Over lunch you could hear the laughter, stories being told and plans for summer break being exchanged among friends.

When lunch was over they all headed out to the playground. Jaxon and his buddies headed to the four square courts to squeeze in one more game before summer break.

"Hey, Carter," said Jaxon. "It's your turn to play." Carter looked up from the bench where he was watching everyone play with a big smile.

"Really?" said Carter as he ran over to Jaxon.

"Yep, it's your turn, buddy," said Jaxon.

You could hear the other kids moaning because they didn't want Carter to play.

"He's too little to play, Jaxon," said one of his friends.

"Third graders aren't allowed to play this game," said another.

Jaxon looked at his friends and said, "Hey guys, Carter

wants a chance to play and I am giving him my spot, so let him play. It's not going to hurt anything and it's the last day of school."

Carter's face was beaming with joy and the other kids respected Jaxon so they let Carter play. It wasn't long before Carter was beat out of the game but he didn't care, for those few minutes playing meant the world to him.

"Good job, buddy," said Jaxon as he gave Carter a high five just as the bell rang.

CHAPTER FOUR

As it was winding down to the end of the day, Mrs. Sappington gave her class the great news that she would also be teaching their 5th grade class next year. The students were very excited, because they loved Mrs. Sappington.

She also gave them a little homework to do over the summer break.

After the moans and groans, Mrs. Sappington got the class to settle down and explained that the homework would be easy and the best one would be placed outside the classroom on a board for one month at the beginning of the school year.

This got their attention and she began to explain what the assignment would be. "I want each of you to write an essay or a story about something that you did over the summer that changed your life for the better. Something that you did that you will never forget. This can be as simple or as detailed as you would like. So, I encourage everyone to submit your paper at the beginning of the school year."

Just then the final bell rang for the year. As Jaxon was getting his backpack off the hanger Mrs. Sappington said, "Jaxon, enjoy your trip to Boston with your family this summer and I'll see you next year!"

Jaxon couldn't wait to go on his trip as this would be his first time flying. "I will, Mrs. Sappington! Maybe something really cool will come out of this trip that I can write about for our homework!" Jaxon said. "See you next year!" He gave a wave and a smile as he headed out the door.

CHAPTER FIVE

Jaxon and his dad drove away chatting about his last day of school, work, and their upcoming vacation to Boston. This would be the first real family vacation they'd taken since Jaxon was born.

Jaxon's mom and dad owned a small construction business that they started several years ago. Jaxon's mom, Ava, did the bookwork for the business and Jaxon's dad, Grant, did the work in the field and bidding of jobs. Jaxon's little sister, Abbygail was 2 years old. Both Jaxon and Abbygail had grown up with the business and ever since Jaxon had been a little guy, he would help his dad work on projects.

Once he started school, Jaxon would spend the summers helping his dad on various job sites. He looked forward to working with his dad each year. This year would be no different, and Jaxon was excited to get home to help his dad get things together to finish a job site before going to their trip.

"Jax, before we head home we need to stop by McGruder's Mercantile to pick up some stain and house numbers for Mr. & Mrs. Percy," said Jaxon's dad as they reached the four-way stop in town.

Jaxon's family had become good friends with Mac McGruder over the years and he had watched the kids grow up. Jaxon loved going in the store because Mr. McGruder was always happy to see him and would let him get a gumball out of the glass jar every time he came to the store. Mr. McGruder knew how to make his customers feel important and this simple gesture made Jaxon feel like a *very* important person... because not everyone got a free gumball.

Before Jaxon's dad went to find the stain he needed, he asked Jaxon to find some house numbers to go on the Percy's house. "Make sure they are something they would like and something that would look good up against cedar siding. You will need two '4's' and one '1,' said Jaxon's dad.

Jaxon took off to find house numbers and came to an aisle that had about 10 different styles of numbers. Jaxon thought about what would look nice and grabbed the appropriate numbers and took them up to the counter.

"Mr. McGruder, do you like this style of house numbers or this style?" said Jaxon pointing at the brushed silver color and the black color numbers he had chosen.

"Which kind do you like, Jaxon?" asked Mr. McGruder

"I think they will like the brushed silver color but I am afraid it won't show up as good on the cedar siding and I think the black is too dull," replied Jaxon.

"Well, come with me young man, I have just what you are looking for," said Mr. McGruder.

Jaxon followed Mr. McGruder to the aisle with all the house numbers and pointed out some house numbers that were brushed silver with a touch of black to make them stand out.

"That's perfect, Mr. McGruder!" exclaimed Jaxon.

Just then Jaxon's dad came up to the two and said, "This is exactly why we shop at McGruder Mercantile; because he has everything we need, including the best advice!"

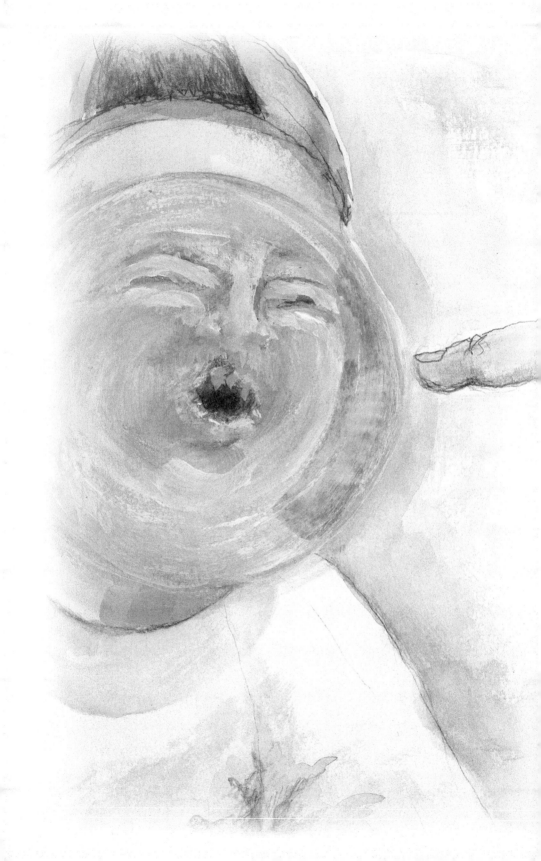

They all three headed up to the checkout counter. Mr. McGruder rang them up and told them to have a great day and come back to see him soon! Jaxon gave a big wave as he blew the biggest grape bubble. Just then, "Pop"!

CHAPTER SIX

That night at dinner Jaxon and his family talked about what needed to get done before they left on vacation. They talked about the different projects that needed a few hours here and there and that they may have to work a little later to get things done. Jaxon was ready to work and didn't mind working late since he would be spending time with his dad learning the trade of construction.

Jaxon was having trouble with math in school. So, his dad started working with him on measurements and Jaxon's math scores got better. When his dad explained things in a language that he understood, it came naturally to Jaxon. When they started learning fractions, Jaxon's dad started working with him right away and made it easier to understand.

"It's the real world experience mixed with what we learn at school that helps us develop skills that we can understand

and use daily," said his dad. "It's my job to encourage you to do your best and to support the decisions you make."

Jaxon understood, and he appreciated the opportunity to get the real world experience he was getting by working with his dad, because not all kids had that opportunity.

"We have to make decisions based on our family and what is best for us," said his mom. "We want to make sure that we have the basics such as a roof over our head and food on the table and the rest is a bonus."

Just then the phone rang and Jaxon's dad answered it. "Yes sir, ok sir, thank you," he said. He turned around to the table.

"Well, it looks like we have some decisions to make as a family," he said as sitting back down at the table. "That was Mr. Pete's son, Charlie. He said that Mr. Pete has fallen and hurt his hip. The only way that Mr. Pete would get to come home would be if his home was safe and he had someone that could check on him daily." This meant that they would have to possibly postpone their trip.

Mr. Pete was their next door neighbor. He had no family or friends close by, other than Grant, Ava, Jaxon and Abbygail James. He never bothered anyone but since Grant and Ava moved in the neighborhood they instantly became good friends. Jaxon would go over a couple times a week and have lemonade after school during the school year, and evenings after Jaxon and his dad got off work during the summer. Mr. Pete was a wonderful older gentleman that really enjoyed the James family and had watched Jaxon and Abbygail grow up.

In December, Mr. Pete had hurt his knee and couldn't get up and down the stairs as swiftly so Jaxon's family pledged to watch over him and help out if they needed to. Mr. Pete was an independent man and could care for himself but in the event he needed something they would be a family he could depend on.

After the family discussed options and what they felt they needed to do to help take care of Mr. Pete they left the ultimate decision up to Jaxon. This was a trip he had waited for his whole life and his parents didn't want to make a decision that would upset him. They talked as a family and agreed to come up with a plan the next evening over dinner. This would give Jaxon enough time to think about what was being decided and to be able to ask questions if he had any. Of course Abbygail would chime in with two year old babbles!

CHAPTER SEVEN

The next morning Jaxon and his dad got up early and headed out to Mr. & Mrs. Percy's house for the day. Grant didn't bring up what they talked about last night as he wanted Jaxon to ask him questions when he was ready. Instead they listened to the radio, told a few jokes and enjoyed spending time together.

"Ok Jaxon, you are going to help me by installing the house numbers on the cedar siding while I stain a few last pieces," said Jaxon's dad. "Grab your tool pouch and let's go on the front porch and I'll show you what needs to be done."

Jaxon grabbed his tool pouch out of his dad's work trailer, then reached in the front seat to get the numbers and headed for the front porch.

"Ok, dad. I'm ready!" said Jaxon.

"I need you to climb up this step ladder and measure 5' 5" from the bottom of the porch down the cedar post and make a small mark with your pencil," said his dad. "Then I need you to measure to the center of the post and add another pencil mark. Your numbers will center on that line, and the top of the first number will touch on the imaginary line at 5' 5" from the bottom of the porch decking up the cedar post. Then, you'll measure 2" from the bottom of the first number to mark the top of the next number. Does that make sense?" said his dad while he was showing him how to get started.

"Yep! But let me repeat it just to make sure I understand how you want it done," said Jaxon. "I will measure 5' 5" from the bottom of the porch down the cedar post and make a mark in pencil. Then I will measure to the center of the post and add another pencil mark, and center my numbers on that line. I'll put the top of the first number on the mark that's 5' 5" from the bottom of the porch, then I will measure 2" from the bottom of the first number to start the top of my next number. Right dad?" he asked.

"That is correct!" his dad said. "Now just be sure the letters are centered, evenly spaced, plumb and level. You remember what plumb and level mean, right, Jaxon?" he asked.

"Plumb means that they are straight up and down and level means they are horizontal making them straight to the eye compared to the placement of the object," he replied.

"Good job Jaxon!" said his dad.

Jaxon began focusing on his task. He began to measure and make small marks on the cedar post, double checking his work. He began to nail in the first number and after one more quick check on his measurements, he nailed the second nail on the number 4. He stood back and looked at it and compared it to the post.

It measured plumb and level and looked good. He moved on to the next number.

He was focusing on his measurements, making sure he had the exact length his dad told him, when his dad slipped around the corner to watch him. He was carefully making sure that he was double checking his work because he knew you must take pride in your work. The work you were doing had to be done correctly or your customers may not ask you to do anything else for them.

His dad couldn't help but smile at the wonderful young man his son was becoming. Jaxon began to nail the number 1 to the post. He did another quick check of the measurements and nailed the final nail in. He got off the ladder and double checked his work. It looked great. "One number to go," he thought. He climbed on the step ladder one more time and measured out the placement of the numbers. He nailed the number 4 perfectly and just as he hopped off the step ladder he caught Mr. Percy watching him.

"You have done a wonderful job with installing those house numbers, Jaxon," he said with a big old smile under his big brimmed hat. "I have been watching you for the last 15 minutes and you have impressed me with your construction skills and knowledge."

Jaxon was pretty proud and his smile showed it. "I'm glad you like it Mr. Percy," he said as he climbed off the porch to get the view Mr. Percy had. "Your siding looks great with a fresh coat of stain and with all of Mrs. Percy's pretty flowers, this place will look awesome!" said Jaxon.

Jaxon cleaned up his mess and went to help his dad finish up his staining project.

"Well, Mr. Percy, I think we are all done with your project. Do you want to walk around with me to make sure we got everything you wanted us to do?" asked Jaxon's dad.

"Sure that would be great, Grant!" said Mr. Percy as he began walking down the stairs on the front porch of his house. He carefully began to look his house over making sure that the work he hired to have done was complete. After several minutes of walking and looking  up and down the side of the house he began to smile then extended his right hand to shake Grant's hand.

"I hired you to do this project because my wife didn't want me out on a ladder and I have to say that it looks better than I imagined. I am very pleased with the work and your professionalism while working on our home. I will have you back out later this fall to work on another part of our home that needs some fixing up."

Mr. Percy leaned over and extended his hand to Jaxon. "Thank you for your hard work too! I know you will make a great construction guy when you get older. You have a perfect example teaching you the right way to do things standing next to you."

Jaxon looked over at his dad and they were both smiling from ear to ear. They exchanged a gentle fist bump.

"Thank you, Mr. Percy, for trusting us with your project. It's a pleasure to work with such great customers like you and Mrs. Percy," said Grant. "Come on Jax, let's get the rest of our things packed up so we can head home and see the girls!"

That night at dinner they talked about what projects they had going on and what the girls did throughout the day. Just as they finished dinner, Ava dished out a fresh peach cobbler complete with homemade vanilla ice-cream for dessert.

"Jaxon, did you happen to decide what you feel we should do about our family vacation?" she asked as she placed his dessert in front of him.

"Yes mom, I've made up my mind," he said with confidence. "I think we need to cancel our trip for now to help Mr. Pete since he needs us. It isn't fair to him for us to leave when we could be just a phone call away."

Ava smiled as she knew this was the best choice. "You always seem to put others before yourself Jaxon, and that's what I love about you!" she said with a warm smile. "Your dad and I promise to take you to Boston at a later date!" Ava said. "Now let's get these dirty dishes to the sink!"

CHAPTER EIGHT

Grant needed some fuel in his truck and pulled into a nearby gas station. As Grant was filling up, Jaxon couldn't help but notice a piece of paper flopping in the wind on a pole near the gas pump. As the wind would flip it one way and back the other way he would catch a glimpse of reds and blues. He tried so hard to figure out what the image was on the flyer but the wind made it nearly impossible.

"Hey dad!" Jaxon yelled. "Can you grab that flyer on the pole next to you, please!" Grant looked at it for a moment and held it still reading it, then lifted the small piece of clear tape that held it on and handed it to Jaxon.

Grant paid for his fuel, grabbed the receipt and hopped in the truck. "So what is the flyer about?" asked Grant as Jaxon was reading it.

"It says, 'Do you know a veteran? Help us take them on a Hero Tour on Friday, September 6th. For more information visit herotour.org.'"

Jaxon looked at his dad and asked, "What's a veteran, dad?"

"Well, a veteran is a man or woman that has served in our military, which ensures, and sometimes fights, for our country and our freedom. When they currently serve our country they are also known as active duty military but when they are discharged or retire they are known as veterans."

Jaxon nodded his head and continued to look at the flyer. "Isn't Mr. Percy a veteran?" asked Jaxon.

"Yes he is, but how did you know that, Jaxon?"

"I saw a sticker on his front window that said WWII Veteran," as Jaxon pointed to the words on the flyer while showing his dad.

"That's a sharp eye you have there, Jaxon! I'm beginning to really wonder what's in that head of yours. Whatever it is, I'm looking forward to getting to know it!"

Later that night Jaxon was lying in bed re-reading the flyer. He heard his mom and dad talking in the living room and wanted to understand more about veterans. He climbed out of bed with the flyer in hand and went down the hallway into the living room.

"Hey buddy, what's up?" asked his mom as she sat up on the couch. Jaxon jumped up on the love seat and curled up in a soft blanket lying nearby.

"I want to know more about veterans," said Jaxon. "I thought a veteran was someone who protects us and our country but is no longer active in serving our country."

Jaxon's dad sat up a little to turn and face him. "You know how we write checks to pay bills for the business? Well someone that signs up for or enlists in the military writes a check too. The difference is the check they write is one that is payable to the United States for an amount up to and including their life."

Jaxon was really focused and listening to his dad and trying to understand what he was saying. "Someone who is currently enlisted in our military can still serve the United States or may be deployed, which means they are serving outside our country and they are considered active duty. When they retire or are discharged from their service they are known as a veteran. The word 'veteran' means they are no longer active duty but are still honored for having done so."

Jaxon finally understood what his dad was saying and he looked down at the flyer in his hand. "Can we look into the information on this flyer because we do know a veteran and I want to know what we can do for him."

Jaxon's mom smiled and said, "I will be more than happy to check into it for you, but for now it's bedtime! You and dad have a busy day tomorrow and you need to get some rest." Jaxon gave his mom and dad a hug and headed off to bed.

CHAPTER NINE

The next morning as Jaxon was gathering his things, his sister was babbling and watching his every move, all the while lining all her Cheerios up on her high chair tray.

"Hey, Jaxon, don't forget your snacks that I sat on the counter for you," his mom said while washing the breakfast dishes.

"Thanks, mom! See you tonight!" said Jaxon.

Jaxon and his dad stopped by the lumberyard to pick up a few things then went by Mr. West's house, which just happened to be down the road from Mr. and Mrs. Percy's house.

"Hey dad, when we get done with our job, can we stop by to say hi to Mr. Percy?" asked Jaxon.

Jaxon's dad just smiled and gave Jaxon's hair a quick tousle and said, "How about later this week? We'll be back around this way on Friday, and we need to get home to the girls!"

That night after dinner, Jaxon's mom grabbed the laptop and asked Jaxon to come sit next to her. She typed in the website from the flyer that Jaxon had brought home. As they both began reading the website, Ava understood the need to find veterans that have served in World War II, Korea and Vietnam to attend a very special flight known as a "Hero Tour" on Friday, September 6th. Jaxon's mom read further to see if there was any specific information that would be important while explaining to Jaxon what this all meant.

"Jaxon," his mom said, "do you understand what this means?" as she pointed to the laptop, showing Jaxon and looking into his eyes.

"Kind of," he said.

"This wonderful organization is dedicated to giving back to our military men and women, specifically those who have served their country many years ago. These wonderful people want to take them to see their respective memorials in Washington, DC." Jaxon really listened to his mom and tried to understand. "The people involved in this organization are all volunteers, which means they get paid nothing while participating in a flight as a way to give thanks to those that have fought for our freedom and protected our country. They do this because it's an honor to be among the true American Heroes known as veterans." Jaxon asked his mom a few questions to clarify this new information that was somewhat foreign to him, but it was obvious that he was really interested in learning more.

"Well buddy, you better brush your teeth and get your pajamas on while I go check on your dad and sissy!" said his mom. As Jaxon headed down the hallway his mom could tell he was excited about the news he just learned about but still had a few questions. He brushed his teeth and climbed in bed waiting for his mom and dad to come tuck him in. His parents walked in to give him a hug and a kiss and as they were leaving he asked, "Mom, can we look at the Hero Tour a little more?"

"Sure buddy, I'll do a little more research and see what I can find out about this organization," his mom said. "Good night Jax, we love you!"

After a few minutes, Jaxon hopped out of bed, grabbed his flashlight and took his piggy bank off his dresser. He poured all of the contents onto his floor and began to count his money. He remembered that he also had some money in his wallet that was in his closet and added that to the pile. With a smile on his face he put the money back in his piggy bank, placed it back on his dresser, turned off his flashlight and climbed back into bed and drifted off to sleep.

CHAPTER ELEVEN

Jaxon's summer was shaping up. He and his dad would go to work and look at a few new jobs to start. Jaxon loved working with his dad as well as interacting with the various customers over his summer break. The best part for him was having the chance to learn the construction trade from someone he loved while earning a little extra cash. Jaxon was really smart about how and when he spent his hard-earned money, and many times would spend it on his little sister or mom just to see them smile. He even bought Carter a new yo-yo from the hardware store because he heard Carter say that he really wanted one.

After dinner Jaxon's mom cleaned off the kitchen table, grabbed her laptop and a pad of paper, and asked Jaxon to come sit down beside her. She had been doing some additional research and wanted to talk to him about it.

"Jaxon, you asked me to find out some additional information about the Hero Tour and I have what you asked for. The Hero Organization was started in 2005. A gentleman had served in World War II and really wanted to see his memorial in Washington, D.C. So. his son flew his personal plane, taking his dad and a couple of his World War II friends on a flight they would never forget. As soon as he got back from this quick trip, he and his buddies began telling their friends. Before they knew it, they had several more veterans that wanted to take this very special trip. So, another group of pilots loaded their private planes with World War II veterans and flew them to Washington, D.C. to see their memorial. As you can see this was the start of something wonderful that began to happen for our veterans."

"Soon they had so many requests that it became apparent there was a need to create a organization in an effort to accommodate not only the veterans wanting to travel on a Hero Tour but serve as the 'home base' as other hubs throughout other states were formed. The Eagle City Hero Tour Organization right here in our hometown was formed in 2009, has taken 40 flights and has taken over 2,500 veterans that have served in World War II, Korea and Vietnam to our Nation's Capital to see their memorials."

Jaxon sat at the island in the kitchen listening carefully to his. After a few moments he began to ask a few questions.

"Mom, how often do they do a Hero Tour?" asked Jaxon.

"That's a great question Jaxon. I don't know. But I will certainly send an e-mail asking any questions that you might have that I can't answer," said his mom.

"I would like to know how much it costs to go on a flight," Jaxon asked.

"Well it says that it is completely free for the veteran to travel on a Hero Tour but a guardian would cost $300.00. The reason it is free of charge to the veterans, is because these men and women have given so much to our country already we feel that this trip should be our grateful thank you. This is possible because of the fundraising efforts of a generous community."

Jaxon's dad stuck his head in the kitchen and said, "Come on buddy, it's time to get ready for bed."

"Thanks, mom, for looking into this for me. Do you think we can talk about it again?" he asked.

"Well, sure we can - but you better listen to your dad and get ready for bed. You boys have a full day of work tomorrow!" she said with a big smile.

"Hey mom, when you e-mail those people can you ask how to get someone signed up, please?" Jaxon said as he jumped off the barstool.

"You bet I will!" said his mom.

Over the next couple weeks Jaxon and his dad worked hard getting some loose ends tied up on a few different jobs and Jaxon never really stopped thinking about the Hero Tour. "Dad," he asked, "you know how Mr. Percy is a veteran?"

"Yep. What's on your mind, Jaxon?"

"I'm thinking about something. Can I talk with you and Mom about it at dinner?"

Just then his dad's cell phone rang. It was his mom letting them know dinner was ready! "Well, I guess that sounds just about perfect!" his dad said.

CHAPTER ELEVEN

That night at the dinner table they talked about the day, what they got done with the projects they had been working on and what the girls did while they were working.

"I think Jaxon has something to talk about," Grant said.

"I have thought about the Hero Tour a lot lately and feel that Mr. Percy needs to go on a flight as a thank you from our community," said Jaxon.

His mom jumped at the thought. "So your sister and I stopped by a garage sale in town. I was making our purchases and noticed the same flyer that you brought home several weeks ago so I decided to ask a few questions that you had asked me," his mom said with Jaxon listening closely.

"It just so happened to be the President of our local Eagle City Hero Tour Organization and after talking to her she

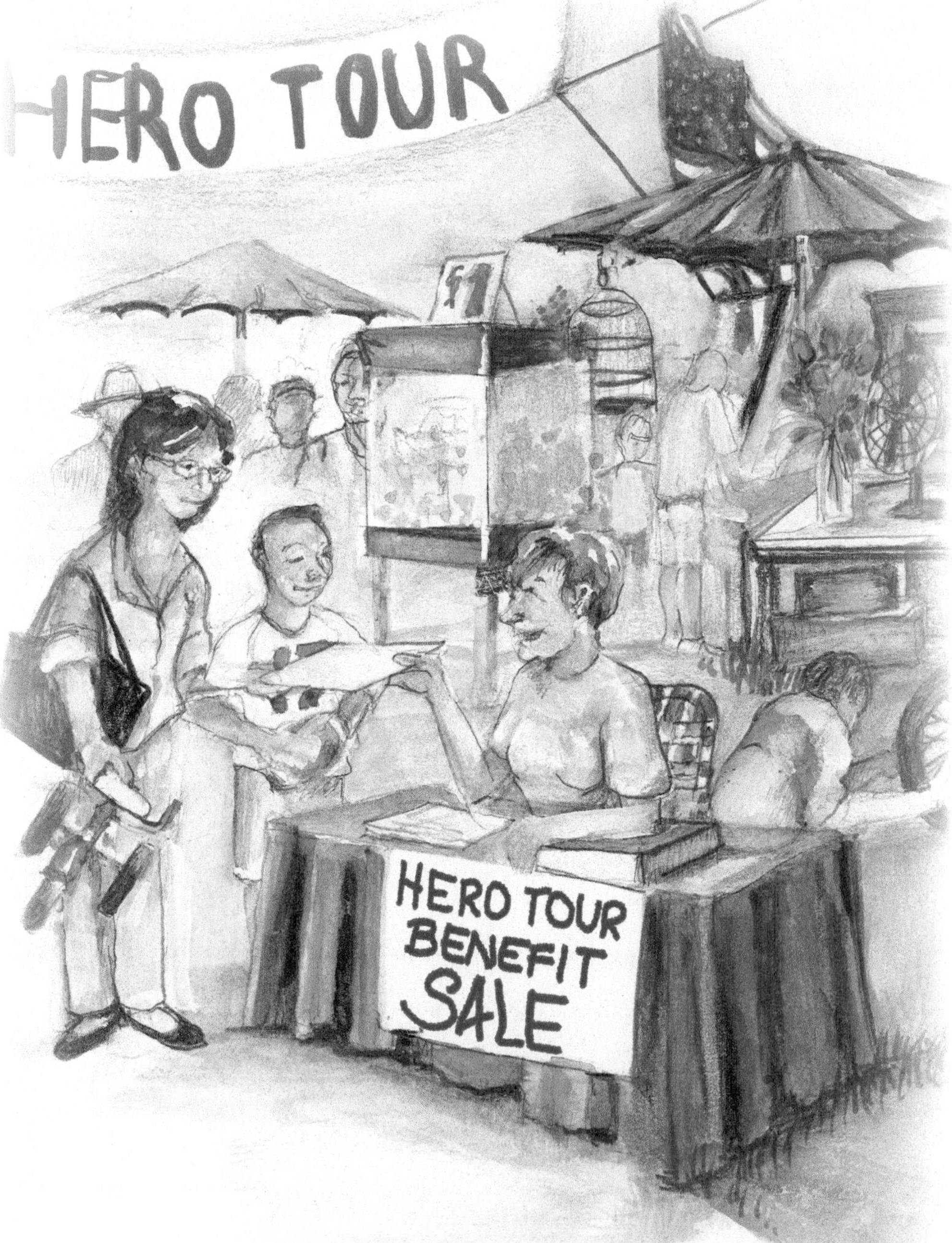
HERO TOUR
$1
HERO TOUR
BENEFIT
SALE

was so excited that you were interested in this organization. She said that they have several hundred fundraisers throughout the year from people of all walks of life, various backgrounds and some of them aren't even from our community. They all do it for the same reason, to give back to our veterans. Because of their generous donations they are able to keep these flights going. There was even a lemonade stand across the street at another garage sale and a set of twins were raising money through the sale of lemonade and duct tape flowers for our Eagle City Hero Tour Organization," his mom said. Jaxon began to smile. You could tell that the kindness of others really meant something to him.

"They have had schools get involved by asking students and staff for pennies throughout the month and raising enough funds to send one veteran on a flight, local food places donating a percentage of their sales, and even a local radio station putting on an event raising enough money to send 50+ veterans on a flight," she said.

"I was really amazed at how much the community does for such a deserving organization and the best part is that 100% of the money goes directly to our veterans," she said. "She also gave me an application and her business card and told me to tell you that you can call her with any questions you might have."

Jaxon's eyes lit up. This was exactly the information that he needed. "Mom and dad, I just wanted to say thank you. You always have time to answer any questions I have had about all of this." Just then, his little sister chimed in with baby babbles and began clapping her little hands.

"It looks like Abbygail feels the same way." They began laughing.

"I would like to talk to Mr. Percy and see if he would be willing to go on a Hero Tour. I have been saving my money for our trip to Boston, but since we weren't able to go I would like to donate money for Mr. Percy to go, and give enough money for another deserving veteran to go as well."

His mom and dad looked at each other and began to smile. They knew their little boy was a caring, compassionate individual who always helped others but this really made them proud. "I counted the money I had saved in my piggy bank and my wallet which was $286.44 and I know I have a little over $400.00 in my savings account at the bank. I would like to take enough out to equal $600.00 and donate," Jaxon said with a serious face. "Those veterans deserve this and if I can help then I want to. It's my way of saying thank you to our veterans."

"Jaxon, let's talk to Mr. Percy and see if he is willing to do this and then we can think about your donation," his dad said.

"Either way I want to help," said Jaxon.

CHAPTER TWELVE

The following week Jaxon called Mr. Percy to see if it was ok if he came over as he has something he would like to talk to him about.

"Well sure you can, Jaxon. Want to come over around 3:00 PM tomorrow?" said Mr. Percy.

"I'll see you at 3:00 PM tomorrow, Mr. Percy! Thanks and I'll talk to you later!" said Jaxon as he hung up the phone.

After the kids went to bed, Ava and Grant talked about life, the kids and just got a chance to catch up.

"That boy of ours is something pretty special," Ava said. "His big heart and willingness to help others is a trait I love."

"He has been asking a lot of questions about this Hero Organization and really feels passionate about donating his hard-earned summer money."

"So what can we do, Grant?" she asked.

"I was wondering the same thing, Ava." he said. "Every year we try to donate to a community organization that gives back and I haven't given anything this year. Perhaps this would the best place to donate in an effort to support Jaxon on something he is learning about as well as give back to those that fight for our freedoms everyday," he said.

"I wonder if it's an option to ask if I could go as Mr. Percy's guardian and ask if Jaxon could go on this trip as well. It would not only be a great opportunity but a great piece of history from the mouths of those that lived it and I would be honored to pay the $300.00 guardian fee for Jaxon and I to go. You said you talked to the President of Eagle City Hero Tour Organization. Can you give me her name so I can ask a few questions myself?"

Ava went to the counter and found the card. "Here you go," she said.

"Thanks! I'll give her a call tomorrow morning."

CHAPTER THIRTEEN

The next morning Jaxon made his way down the hallway to the kitchen. His mom and dad were talking and getting Abbygail ready for breakfast. "Hey buddy, I need to run down to the store to pick up a few things so we can get our day started. I'll be back in a bit to pick you up," his dad said.

Jaxon was still a little sleepy and rubbed his eyes and gave a big stretch. "Ok dad, I'll play with Abbygail until you get back," he said.

"Once you get done with your breakfast, of course," his mom said smiling as she set his plate on the table.

"Mrs. Pauley, this is Grant James. My wife talked to you last week about the Hero Tour and our son, Jaxon was asking several questions about it," he said.

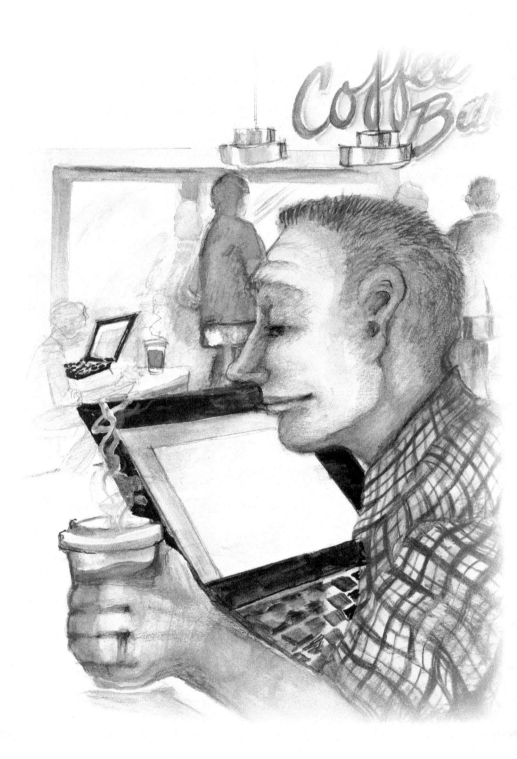

"Oh yes, I so enjoyed talking to your wife and I told her to please call with any questions," she said.

"Well, Jaxon has pitched to us that he would like to pay for 2 veterans to go on a Hero Tour. He has been working with me all summer and has saved up his birthday money and money from various jobs and would like to pay it forward. He wants to ask a World War II veteran that we have done a lot of work for over the years, and I would like to inquire about possibly being his guardian," he said. "I would also like to know if it is possible if Jaxon could go on this trip, and I would be happy to pay the $300.00 guardian fee for him as well. We were going to take a family trip to Boston this year but our plans got cancelled. Once he saw your flyer he has been so interested in finding out additional information about this organization, and although he has not asked to go on this trip I would like to surprise him by allowing him to travel with some true American Heroes to learn about history far richer than any text book," he said.

"Wonderful! First, you will need to fill out an application for yourself to serve as a guardian. We have a process that we have to follow to make sure that we are choosing the most appropriate and qualified individuals traveling with us on our flights. While I can't make any promises I will tell you that I will give serious consideration to allowing Jaxon to go. This is not something we normally do as this isn't a vacation but rather we make this trip about our veterans. If you will get the veteran application and the guardian application turned in very soon, we will get them reviewed and get back to you," she said.

"Thank you for your time, Mrs. Pauley, I'll talk to you soon." Grant hung up the phone, smiled quietly to himelf and headed out to his truck.

Shortly after this phone call, Grant stopped by the coffee shop to plug in his laptop and log onto the website and read through all the various information about guardians and their responsibilities and expectations. He printed out a guardian application, filled it out in its entirety as well as an application for Jaxon and submitted them via e-mail to Mrs. Pauley along with a short note that read:

> "Mrs. Pauley, I wanted to thank you for taking time to talk to me about the Hero Tour. I do understand that you don't normally allow children on flights. However in the event you allow an exception I have submitted an application for Jaxon, along with my application. Jaxon is going to Mr. Percy's house this afternoon to ask him if he would be interested in attending a Hero Tour. Jaxon is going to offer to pay the $300.00 to send Mr. Percy on this flight as

well as enough to send one more veteran of your choosing in an effort to pay it forward. Jaxon doesn't know that I have talked to you, however, he will be contacting you in the next couple days. Again, thank you for your time and consideration."

—Grant James.

CHAPTER FOURTEEN

"Jaxon, your dad just pulled back in the driveway so grab your things," his mom said. Jaxon kissed his sister and gave his mom a quick hug and headed out the door.

"Hey buddy, don't forget Mr. Percy's veteran application," she said as she quickly walked to the front door with the application in hand.

"Thanks mom!" Jaxon said as he tucked it in his backpack and jumped up into the truck.

With the windows rolled down Jaxon and his dad headed across town to Mr. Percy's house. Grant couldn't help but smile as he looked over and saw the sunshine on Jaxon's face and the wind blowing in his hair. *How did our baby boy grow up so fast,* he wondered.

Just then they pulled into Mr. Percy's driveway. Mr. & Mrs. Percy were sitting out on the porch enjoying the beautiful day and waiting for Jaxon to show up! Just then Mr. Percy looked down at his watch, "Well Jaxon you are 5 minutes early!" he said with a big smile. Grant shook Mr. Percy's hand and gave Mrs. Percy a hug. Jaxon quickly followed in his dad's footsteps.

"Let's go inside and get a soda pop!" said Mr. Percy. "You boys have a seat at the table and I'll get your drinks," said Mrs. Percy.

"Mr. Percy, I have heard about an organization and wanted to see if it's something you would be interested in being a part of," said Jaxon.

"Oh you think so?" said Mr. Percy.

"Yes, sir. You see I saw a flyer at the gas station several weeks ago and it said if you know of a World War II veteran please visit a website to learn more information. I asked my mom and dad to help me figure out why they wanted World War II veterans and it's because they have a Hero Tour." Jaxon said as he presented his pitch to Mr. Percy.

Mr. Percy sat quietly and listened as Jaxon explained what exactly a Hero Tour was and how it was created, with the help of his dad. "Mr. Percy, I have saved my birthday money and money I have made from working over the summer and school breaks and I would like to send you on a Hero Tour. I was going to use my money for vacation but since our neighbor Mr. Pete got hurt and needed us to help out, we cancelled our vacation. I couldn't think of a better person or organization to donate my money to as you have served our country proudly," he said with heartfelt thanks and appreciation.

Mr. Percy sat there for a few minutes to soak in everything Jaxon had told him. "Jaxon, I can't thank you enough for thinking of me. But, I am 94 years old and I haven't flown in 40 years or more. Why don't you give me a day or two to think about this. I'll call my doctor to make sure he is ok with me flying," said Mr. Percy.

Jaxon seemed disappointed that Mr. Percy didn't immediately say yes and Grant could see it in his son's eyes. "Jaxon, let's head back home to the girls and we'll check in with Mr. Percy in a couple days." as he gave Jaxon's hair a quick tousle. "Mr. Percy, Mrs. Percy, thank you so much for taking time to talk to Jaxon. You both enjoy your evening and we'll talk to you soon," said Grant. "Jaxon, don't forget to give a handshake to Mr. Percy and a hug to Mrs. Percy. With the application still lying on the table, Mr. & Mrs.

Percy warmly accepted Jaxon's handshake and hug and they waved goodbye.

On the way home Grant could tell something was bothering Jaxon. "Buddy, what's wrong?" his dad said as he turned down the radio.

"I just don't know why Mr. Percy didn't say yes," he said as he shrugged his shoulders.

"Jaxon, sometimes it's best to think about things for a couple days instead of immediately saying yes or no. I think you surprised him by asking him to go on a Hero Tour including donating your own money to send him. That is such a kind gesture and I am so proud of you. You also have to understand that his service to our country was a long time ago. It's not something that many veterans often talk about," his dad said.

"Remember when we were planning our vacation and originally we wanted to go to Arizona but it just didn't work out so we chose to go to Boston instead?" his dad asked. Jaxon looked at his dad and nodded his head. "Well, it's a good thing we didn't book that trip to Arizona because we would have had to cancel it due to a really bad storm that was headed that way. It's the same thing; Mr. Percy didn't want to tell you yes and then have to cancel on you. I promise you that things will work out the way they're supposed to. You just have to have a positive attitude and be patient," his dad said with a smile.

Jaxon understood what his dad was saying and, although the hardest part is waiting, he was willing to give Mr. Percy the time he needed to make a decision.

CHAPTER FIFTEEN

The next morning the phone rang.

"I'm sorry he isn't here right now but I'll be happy to give him a message. Thank you and have a great day, too," said Ava. After she got Abbygail cleaned up and ready to go to town she went to Grant and gave him a couple messages from earlier phone calls.

"Hey Jaxon." his dad said. "When we get done picking up our tools and materials from this job site, mom had a message that Mr. Percy wants you to stop by." Jaxon gave his dad a huge grin and began gathering items and placing them in the truck and trailer.

As they pulled into Mr. Percy's driveway he was waiting outside for them.

"Jaxon, I have given a lot of thought to this Hero Tour," said Mr. Percy. Jaxon listened very carefully. "I have decided that

I would like to go and here is the application that you left on my kitchen table." Jaxon lit up. "Thank you so much Mr. Percy," Jaxon said. "I can't tell you how much this means to me. I will turn this in and contact you when I hear back from the Eagle City Hero Tour Organization."

He was so happy that Mr. Percy was willing to take this very special flight and couldn't wait to get it turned into Mrs. Pauley to get him on the waiting list.

"Mom! Mom! Mom!" Jaxon yelled as he ran inside. "You are never going to believe this! Mr. Percy agreed to go on the Hero Tour and here's his application!" he said with excitement.

His mom looked at his dad and smiled. "Well, it sounds like we need to get a cover letter written and submit his application to Mrs. Pauley! I would like for you to come into the kitchen and start writing a letter that will give the Hero Tour organization information about your veteran that we can send along with his application. I'll get dinner going," said his mom. Jaxon went to his room and grabbed a note pad and pencil. He sat himself at the table and began thinking about what he wanted to say.

Dear Mrs. Pauley,

My name is Jaxon James and I am going to be a 5th grader at Eagle Ridge Elementary School. I found one of your flyers at a local gas station and after learning about the Eagle City Hero Tour Organization I have found a wonderful veteran that I would like to get on your waiting list for an upcoming Hero Tour. Attached is the application for Lt. Col. F. Percy who served during World War II. I would like to send you $300.00 for him to go on a flight, as well as an additional $300.00 for another veteran of your choosing to go on a flight. They fought for our country and our freedom and it would be an honor to give back to them. Thank you for your time and I look forward to hearing from you.

Sincerely,

Jaxon James

"Ok Mom, I think I have my cover letter ready," said Jaxon.

"Perfect! After dinner I will take you to the bank at the mall since they stay open until 7:00 PM. We'll get a Cashier's Check and mail out your cover letter, application and donation tomorrow. Now, if you will please clean off the table and wash your hands then dinner is almost ready!" his mom said. "Grant, Abbygail... dinner is ready!" she said as she peeked her head in the living room.

CHAPTER SIXTEEN

After dinner, Jaxon and his mom gathered the money from his piggy bank and wallet and headed to the bank while his dad and Abbygail stayed home. At the teller window Jaxon handed her the baggie full of his money and change. "I need to get a $600.00 Cashier's Check please. There should be $286.44 and I will need to withdraw $313.56 out of my savings account," he said with his mom right by his side.

"Give me just a few minutes to count the change," said the teller. After a few moments she came back to the counter. "Who would you like this check made payable to and who is it from?" she asked.

"It's from Jaxon James and made payable to Eagle City Hero Tour Organization please," he said.

Within a few minutes she handed him the check. "Have a great day!" she said.

"You too!" Jaxon and his mom said as they walked outside.

Once they got back home Jaxon grabbed an envelope and addressed it to Eagle City Hero Tour Organization, entered his return address and placed a stamp on it. He placed his cover letter, Mr. Percy's application, and the cashier's check inside the envelope and sealed it shut. Tomorrow they would run it by the post office.

A week went by. He and his dad just happened to stop by the house to pick up a couple things one afternoon. "Hey Jaxon," his mom said with a big smile. "I have a letter for you."

"You do?" Jaxon asked as he took the piece of mail off the counter. It was from the Eagle City Hero Tour Organization and he quickly opened it. Inside there was a letter that read:

> Dear Jaxon,
>
> I wanted to say thank you for the nice letter, veteran application and the generous donation of $600.00 to send two veterans on a Hero Tour. We have contacted Lt Col. F.A. Percy to let him know that he would be going

on a Hero Tour Friday September 6th. We have selected your father to serve as Mr. Percy's guardian on this flight and it would be our honor to have you serve as his junior guardian on this flight as well. We feel that your work ethic and passion towards helping our veterans would be fitting to serve in this role. Your father graciously paid the fee for the both of you to go on this flight. If you accept, we will see you Friday September 6th at 5:00 AM.

Sincerely,

Mrs. Millie Pauley

President, Eagle City Hero Tour Organization

Jaxon was so excited! His parents had received a call prior to receiving the letter and they were just as excited for Jaxon, as well as Grant having the opportunity to serve as Mr. Percy's guardian on this very special trip. The rest of the day Jaxon was pumped. To receive news that Mr. Percy would be going on this flight was awesome. To receive news that his dad would serve as his guardian was really cool but for Jaxon to be asked to be a part of this flight was truly an honor. The next couple of days, Jaxon found it hard to focus and couldn't wait to spend time with Mr. Percy.

CHAPTER SEVENTEEN

On September 6th, they arrived at the hotel where the group was meeting. There were many volunteers and veterans already in the lobby. Grant and Jaxon walked over to the guardian table to get items they would need for the day, including their name badges.

Just then Mr. & Mrs. Percy in the door, as she was going to see her husband off, and also wanted to see Grant and Jaxon this morning. Jaxon gave Mr. Percy a handshake and Mrs. Percy a hug. "Now you take good care of Mr. Percy today," she said.

"We will, I promise!" said Jaxon as his dad was smiling and giving a nod. Mr. Percy gave a hug and a peck on the cheek to Mrs. Percy. In their 62 years together they had only spent a handful of days apart. "I'll see you late tonight," said Mr. Percy.

As they walked into a conference room they were serving breakfast for those traveling on today's flight. Mr. Percy sat down at a table and saved a seat for Grant and Jaxon while Grant made a plate of scrambled eggs, bacon, biscuits and gravy and some fresh fruit for Mr. Percy. Jaxon got Mr. Percy a coffee and some creamer. Once all veterans were through the line then it was time for the guardians. Grant and Jaxon waited in line for their turn but always kept an eye on Mr. Percy.

After breakfast there was a meeting for all guardians on the flight. This was a routine meeting and a way for staff and medical personnel traveling on today's flight to communicate anything that needed to be addressed without the veterans knowing or being embarrassed.

"There will be a total of 110 people on today's flight: 7 World War II veterans, 23 Korean War veterans and 27 Vietnam veterans. The rest is made up of guardians, medical staff and one junior guardian, Jaxon James," said Sterling Pauley. Sterling was the brother of Mrs. Pauley, the president of

Eagle City Hero Tour Organization and was serving as the flight director for this flight. "We'll be taking plenty of wheelchairs on this flight, as the distance that we will cover today some of the veterans may get tired and safety is the number one concern for today. As we embark on this trip, I need to make sure everyone is 100% on board and ready to show our veterans one of the best trips of their lives. Today they will be treated like VIP's, as they are taken nearly 1,500 miles from home, visiting various memorials, including our national cemetery, and then coming back home to their loved ones safe and sound," he said. "There will be times that you will be asked to help with a veteran, and possibly a job you weren't aware of or may not have been given, but we will all team together to make sure these true American Heroes feel appreciated, honored and loved." He talked a little more about today's schedule and things that they would be seeing and that they needed for everyone to work together. "The goal is to get our veterans to each of the places on the itinerary and back to the airport to catch our flight home safely."

Stella Pauley was the wife of Sterling and would serve as the co-flight director and logistics coordinator for this flight. She would make sure that the group got to the various locations on the trip at certain times to stay on track. She gave out instructions to each guardian regarding the care for the veteran they were paired with, and what bus they would be on for the day.

"We have 2 buses in order to accommodate the 110 of us going on this Hero Tour today. The front bus will be known as the "Red Bus" and the bus in the back will be known as the "Blue Bus." If you look down at your nametag inside your lanyard you will notice it is in either red ink or blue ink and that tells you what bus you will be on. If you ever have any questions, don't be afraid to ask. Now let's go back and get our veterans ready to board the buses!" she said with a warm smile.

As everyone began boarding the buses, Mr. Percy sat next to another veteran while Jaxon and Grant sat next to each other. Mr. Percy immediately began striking up a conversation with this gentleman. As they left on the short 30 minute drive to the airport, the many volunteers that had been checking everyone in and helping with breakfast lined up on the sidewalk and waved goodbye to the buses.

This would be a trip to remember.

CHAPTER EIGHTEEN

As they arrived at the airport, the buses began unloading. Guardians gathered their backpacks and paired back up with their veterans while making their way to the security checkpoint. After they got everyone through the security checkpoint and made their way down to the gate to board the plane, the lady who was working at the gate made an announcement over the entire airport.

"Ladies and gentlemen, I would like to direct your attention to gate H7 and help me give a warm welcome to the local Eagle City Hero Tour Organization. They are getting ready to take nearly 60 veterans, who served in World War II, Korea and Vietnam, on a Hero Tour, and are taking them to our Nation's Capital to see their memorials."

The entire airport erupted into clapping and cheering as a token of their appreciation and thanks to those veterans.

Jaxon looked over at Mr. Percy and grinned. Mr. Percy winked back. Grant couldn't help but smile as he brought Mr. Percy another cup of coffee.

They begin boarding the plane and Mr. Percy sat in the front row with a couple of other veterans that he had gotten to know on the bus, while Grant and Jaxon sat on the next row behind them along with another guardian. The flight attendant did her final count and closed the door on the plane.

Just then both the pilot and co-pilot stepped outside the cockpit and addressed the passengers of the entire plane.

"On behalf of Five-Star Airlines, I am Major Kristen Franklin and this is my co-pilot, Captain Erika Shortfield. We would like to say thank you for your service to our country. We have both served our country's military proudly and it's both an honor and a privilege to take you on this flight. Sit back, relax and enjoy the 2 hour 45 minute flight to Washington, D.C." They gave a quick wave and headed back into the cockpit. It wasn't long until they were on the runway and ready to take off.

Jaxon sat in the middle seat between his dad and another guardian.

"Hi there big guy, my name is Garrett Blake but everyone calls me GB!" He could see that Jaxon was a little nervous. "Have you ever flown before, Jaxon?" asked GB.

"No sir! This is my very first flight and I am so excited to serve as a junior guardian today with my dad!" said Jaxon.

"Well, I hope you are ready for a flight to remember because each one of these Hero Tours certainly makes you appreciate our military men and women even more. This day is full of emotions for all of us and I hope you enjoy spending this very rare opportunity with so many of our true American heroes!" GB said with a smile. Jaxon avidly listened to what GB was saying and couldn't wait to experience this special day with everyone.

Mr. Percy sat by the window of the airplane. The veteran that he was talking to was also a World War II veteran. They hit it off and didn't stop talking the whole flight. It was hard to hear them but it was obvious that they had similar stories and had served in similar places.

Jaxon and Grant learned so much about the Eagle City Hero Tour Organization and the flights they take while talking to GB. GB had been on 20 of the 40 flights taken since this local Hero Organization was created. He was great about

answering questions for Jaxon and Grant while explaining a
little about why he got involved in this organization. During
their conversation they learned that GB was drafted into the
Army had served in the Vietnam war from 1967-1968. He
was known as the "Ammo Sergeant" and was responsible
for getting ammo to the firing artillery unit. Jaxon thought
that was pretty cool!

It made the almost 3-hour flight "fly" by! Soon they were
descending, and preparing to land.

CHAPTER NINETEEN

After a few more announcements were made, they landed and were heading towards the terminal when they saw that the local Washington D.C. Fire Department was standing outside their trucks saluting the plane and spraying the airplane with water as it was taxiing in. Clapping and cheering broke out on the plane as this was a really special and unexpected gesture to welcome this flight to Washington, D.C.

As they began getting off the plane row by row, there was a ground crew from the local Washington D.C. Hero Tour Organization there to help. They knew how important these flights were to our veterans and they wanted to make sure they could help in any way to make the Eagle City Hero Tour's flight time in Washington, D.C. the best that it could be.

As everyone came up the jetway you could hear clapping and cheering again. Once veterans made it to the top of the jetway and entered the airport there were young cadets and service men and women in full uniform waiting in a long line to shake their hands. The general public was standing up waving American flags and clapping as the veterans made their way to the ground transportation shuttle area. Grant looked down at Jaxon and you could tell that this kind gesture took him by surprise. With tears in his eyes he looked at his dad and gave him a big smile. Jaxon was pushing Mr. Percy in a wheelchair, as that would be the safest and easiest way to get him around the memorials throughout the day. As they were getting ready to board the buses, Mr. Percy looked at Jaxon and Grant and said, "Wow, I sure didn't expect that! What a nice surprise from so many strangers."

They loaded the buses and headed towards the World War II memorial. The bus driver took them on a tour of downtown Washington, D.C. to show some of the cities highlights as well as giving a history lesson on the various buildings, statues and noteworthy sites. The bus driver really knew his history and was great at telling interesting stories.

As the buses pulled up to the World War II memorial, they couldn't help but notice about 200 middle school students lined up, creating a path into the entrance of the memorial. They were holding American flags and signs they had made with each veterans names and various patriotic messages welcoming this Hero Tour. This was a wonderful surprise especially once they saw their names on the poster boards they were holding. As the veterans made their way to the memorial the students shook their hands and gave hugs or handshakes to each one of them.

Mr. Percy was taken back by this gesture and couldn't believe the students were there waiting for them. He couldn't help but have a warm smile on his face! A couple of the teachers of these classes came over to a small group of veterans and guardians to thank them for their service and to let them know that a couple of the students came up with this suggestion when planning for their class field trips. This was a great way to not only welcome this Hero Tour but for the students to be able to learn about the history of the World War II memorial while being able to spend some time with the men and women who served in World War II.

Grant began pushing Mr. Percy in a wheelchair around the memorial while Jaxon walked next to Mr. Percy. Jaxon knew this memorial meant a lot to Mr. Percy and he couldn't wait to explore all the quotes that were inside this beautiful

granite memorial. As they made it all the way around the inside of the memorial, Grant stopped several times to get photos of Mr. Percy and Jaxon. Mr. Percy would want to show Mrs. Percy where they visited. He wouldn't be able to tell her about their trip without some great photos!

"Look Mr. Percy, it says Missouri on the wall! You should get a picture in front of that since that is our home state!" Jaxon said. Mr. Percy gave a quick nod yes and Grant pushed him up the incline, and locked the wheels on his wheelchair so that Mr. Percy could stand up. Mr. Percy and Jaxon smiled for the photo.

"Let's take one of just Mr. Percy," said Grant has he motioned Jaxon to step aside to capture Mr. Percy's photo. "Perfect! Now let's get you back into the wheelchair so we can get back over to the front of the memorial for a photo," said Grant.

Sterling was motioning everyone to gather in the center of the two water fountains for a group photo. Mr. Percy wanted to stand for this photo and with Grant and Jaxon's help made his way over to the crowd of veterans. They were getting directions from the Eagle City Hero Tour photographer, Annette.

"Ok I need everyone to look this direction and smile for me." She said in a cheerful and loud voice so that everyone could hear. "Awesome job everyone! Thank you!"

As quickly as they gathered to take the group photo they would be asked to head back to the buses with their guardians as they had other memorials to visit.

"Can I ask our seven World War II veterans to hang tight as we would like to get a photo of *just* you at your memorial," said Sterling. The veterans regrouped, took the picture, and headed for the buses.

Over the next several hours they had the chance to visit many of the various memorials including the Korean War Memorial, and the Vietnam Veterans Memorial, while visiting Washington, D.C.

Another really cool thing they got a chance to do was visit the Arlington National Cemetery where they witnessed the Changing of the Guard at the Tomb of the Unknown Soldier. Sterling and Stella gave their buses some ground rules for visiting this very special presentation that they were about to witness.

"We ask that you please leave your cell phone on the bus so that there isn't any chance of it ringing during this presentation," Stella said. "We also have to be very quiet, with no talking, as this is showing our respect. One really special thing just for our Hero Tour is that when the soldiers are done and they begin to walk away you will hear a scuffing of metal from the bottom of their shoe on the concrete. That is to honor each of our veterans here today," said Sterling.

As the buses began unloading, veterans and guardians made their way to stand on the concrete stairs or sit in their wheelchairs so that everyone would be able to see. For the next several minutes it was so quiet you could hear a pin drop.

What they witnessed was nothing short of amazing. In between each pause was a very calculated and precise 21. 21 steps, 21 second pause and 21 steps repeated many times over the course of an hour until they changed guards again. In the military 21 is the highest honor, which is why you hear a 21 gun salute at a military funeral. 21 is also the sum of the numbers of the year of our country's independence, 1776.

Just before boarding the buses Annette wanted to take one more group photo. With the help of Sterling and Stella,

Annette was ready to capture their photo. "This time can I have everyone salute please," she said in a loud and very cheerful voice. "Thank you all so much!"

"Before you board the bus I wanted to let you know that across the driveway is the World War II's most decorated veteran's grave. If you would like to stop by to see it or even for a quick photo we ask that you make your way over there. Your guardians would be happy to help with any photos you wish to take," said Sterling.

"Let's plan to be heading to the buses in 15 minutes as our next stop is the airport to head home!" said Stella.

This certainly was a long day and although everyone was tired they were so happy to have been a part of this trip. Many of the veterans really enjoyed their day and they couldn't believe everything they had seen and experienced. It was great seeing them telling stories and talking about their experiences and memories from years ago. The guardians were so kind and helpful to the veterans they were assigned to assist.

CHAPTER TWENTY

As the buses unloaded at the airport, veterans and guardians were greeted by a ground crew welcoming them. They made their way through airport security and sat down at the gate to wait for their plane to arrive. Everyone was given a ticket for their meal and there were 10 different food locations within this wing of the airport to choose from.

"Mr. Percy, what would you like to eat for supper?" asked Jaxon with his dad nearby.

"What do you guys say we go get a hamburger and fries?" said Mr. Percy

"That sounds like a plan," said Grant has he wheeled Mr. Percy down the food court area. Jaxon found a table and made sure it was easy for his dad to park the wheelchair Mr. Percy was using. After all he wanted to sit next to Mr. Percy for supper.

"We've got 2 hamburgers, 1 cheeseburger, 3 orders of fries and 3 sodas for table number 23!" said the counter staff. Jaxon went up to get their supper and noticed a veteran from their flight was still waiting for his meal.

"Sir, I have noticed that you have been waiting awhile. What did you order for supper?" he asked

"Just a cheeseburger and fries," said the veteran.

"Why don't you come sit over here by us and I'll give you my cheeseburger and fries and when yours is done I'll take it?" Jaxon said with a smile.

"Are you sure?" asked the veteran.

"Of course I am! What is your name, sir?" Jaxon said as he stuck out his hand to offer a handshake.

"My name is Harlan Mueller." He said with a firm handshake.

"Dad and Mr. Percy, this is Mr. Mueller," Jaxon said as Mr. Percy turned his head to give a look.

"Well, so we meet again!" said Mr. Percy. Just a few minutes into their conversation a nice young lady came and brought a cheeseburger, fries and 4 milkshakes to their table.

"I'm so sorry for the delay in getting your food. Our manager asked me to tell you thank you for your service, and to give you and your companions these shakes with our compliments," she said in the most sincere voice.

After supper they headed back to the gate to wait with the rest of their group. It was as if the Hero Tour took over this wing of the airport with everyone wearing matching shirts, backpacks everywhere and veterans reflecting on this fast paced yet memorable day. Just then an announcement was made from one of the employees

"Ladies and gentleman, flight 3940 from Washington, D.C. at gate 4 will be boarding in the next 5 minutes. I would like to take a moment to wish this very special flight a safe trip home as this flight has some very special World War II, Korean War and Vietnam veterans on board. They have spent most of today here in Washington, D.C. visiting their memorials. If it wasn't for these courageous men and women we wouldn't have the freedoms we have today," she said with a soft and gentle voice.

The airport began to clap and cheer and several people at nearby gates came over to shake the hands of many veterans. Jaxon looked at his dad with a big smile. Grant knew this day really had a positive impact on not only Jaxon but everyone involved.

CHAPTER TWENTY ONE

It was nearly 10:00 PM when they arrived to the airport back home. It was dark, and as the guardians began taking each of the veterans down the ramp onto the concrete they noticed that this was no ordinary trip home. There were hundreds of motorcycle riders, firefighters, police cadets, family members, and military men and women all lined up holding flags and signs to welcome these true American heroes home. There were certainly tears of joy from so many, as this was not the welcome home they received many years ago when they came home from the service.

There were bagpipes and drums playing in the distance as each of the veterans names were read off as they began to enter the airport. It really was an exciting time and a perfect ending to an incredible trip to remember.

Mr. Percy wanted to walk from the plane to the airport entrance so with Jaxon on one side and Grant on the other,

hand in hand, they made their way to Mrs. Pauley, the President of the Eagle City Hero Tour Organization. With the biggest smile and loudest voice she announced,

"Mr. F.A. Percy a World War II Marine Pilot, Welcome Home!" Mr. Percy gently squeezed both of their hands before saluting Mrs. Pauley.

Just as he got inside the front door of the airport, Mrs. Percy was waiting for him. He gave her the biggest hug, the cutest kiss on the lips and turned around to make room for Jaxon and Grant to give hugs to Mrs. Percy.

Grant asked if one of the volunteers nearby would take their picture. They squeezed in and grabbed a quick photo before Grant went to get the truck to take everyone home. Mr. Percy gave Jaxon the biggest hug and the warmest "Thank you."

CHAPTER TWENTY TWO

A few days went by and the phone rang.

"Jaxon, this is Mr. Percy," a familiar voice on the other line said. "When you and your dad have a moment I want you to stop by the house so I can show you something."

Jaxon was really excited, as he wanted to talk to Mr. Percy once they got back from their trip, just to catch up on what they both thought and show some of the pictures they had taken while in Washington, D.C.

Later that evening Jaxon and Grant stopped by Mr. & Mrs. Percy's house. Mrs. Percy had some of her famous chocolate chip cookies and glasses of milk waiting for them at the table. As they sat at the dining room table talking about their trip Jaxon wanted to know how Mr. Percy got into the military.

"Well, I was a little boy growing up on our family's farm not far from here. When I was about 5 years old I remember standing in the yard while my mother was putting clothes on the line and seeing an airplane. I was so impressed with airplanes that I told my mother I wanted to fly one when I was older."

"When I was younger and in grade school, I was one of four kids that got to school by riding my horse. In Spring of 1941, the college I attended accepted a contract to train pilots and I signed up to be trained in this program."

"I had accepted three different contracts, 1. Primary 2. Secondary and 3. Cross Country Flights. I completed all of those contracts and at age 19, I enlisted in the military as a Naval Aviation Cadet. In March 1942 I became commissioned and taught flight duty, gunnery, communication and aerobatics before teaching ground carrier training. I had to teach students how to take off and land on a ground carrier that was located in the ocean."

"In 1943 I was selected to become a Marine and was a 2nd Lieutenant fighter pilot. When you are a fighter pilot you are also your own flight crew which means that you are responsible for your own plane. As a pilot you are also the mechanic, navigator, gunner and decision maker."

"After about 3 months I became the division leader over 14 guys. My very favorite plane to fly was the Corsair F4U. Boy, that thing flew like a dream!" Mr. Percy said with a laugh.

Jaxon was really engaged and wanted to hear more.

"I was part of the Gilbert Island Group and in June 1944 I was shot down in my Corsair F4U seen in this picture just off Wotje about 68 nautical miles from land. The oil cooler in the hub of the right wing was hit and all the engine oil bled out and the engine froze. I had to glide about 12,000 feet and land into the ocean. My wing man, John, was circling me until a Navy Destroyer picked me up."

"Oh and you remember Mr. Mueller that went on our flight?" asked Mr. Percy as Jaxon and Grant both shook their heads yes. "Mr. Mueller and I were talking about what we did during service and I found out that Mr. Mueller was a submariner who was in that exact same area when I was shot down! How wild is that?" Mr. Percy asked with a laugh "His job was to protect us from the Japanese submarines."

"They took me to Roi-Namur to get medical attention and I was out flying again the next day. In August, 1945 I was flying low over Kyushu, Japan while escorting Navy P2V on August 2nd or 3rd, 1945 and my plane was hit again.

Shrapnel went into the belly of the plane and hit me in the legs and face." He pointed to his face, and said, "This is why I have scars on the right side of my nose, chin and lip. The medics left the shrapnel in my lower leg because they didn't want to mess with my bones. Over the years it worked it's way out of my leg."

"When World War II was over I served in the Reserves and had 2 weeks of active duty and flew once a month. I retired after 23 years in the military on July 1, 1964. It was an honor to serve our military and when they offered me the full Colonelship position I turned it down because I didn't want to sit behind a desk and give orders. I would rather be flying and serving with my men," he said with a heartfelt voice.

"Hang on one moment, I have something to show you."

After a few moments he came back into the room with a small box. Inside were several boxes, photos and papers.

"These are awards and medals I earned during my military career," he said while opening several of the boxes. "These things really don't mean much to me because I was just doing my job and I enjoyed flying," he explained while trying to find something else and shuffling through this box.

"What are those 5 boxes Mr. Percy?" asked Jaxon

"Those are 5 air medals I received during my service, and let me tell you that it was really tough to earn one of these medals as you had to do something really impressive for the Operations Officer of your Squadron to put in a recommendation to receive one," Mr. Percy said with a serious face.

"Can I see them Mr. Percy?" asked Jaxon.

"Well sure you can!" Mr. Percy said, opening each box.

"This one was earned while in Tarawa which is part of the Gilbert Islands; Kwajalein Atoll which is part of the Marshall Islands; Roi-Namur which is part of the Marshall Islands; Okinawa, Japan and Kyushu, Japan."

Jaxon and Grant were so amazed at this story Mr. Percy was telling them, and they couldn't believe they never knew much about his service with all the projects they have done for Mr. & Mrs. Percy over the years.

"What is in this box, Mr. Percy?" asked Jaxon.

"That is my Purple Heart," said Mr. Percy. "I received that last year for the plane crash that I survived, and received a second one from when I survived my plane being shot and shrapnel went into my body."

"Here it is!" Mr. Percy said as he held up a long skinny piece of bronze-like metal. "These are my pilots' wings."

"Woah that's so cool!" said Jaxon. "Can I hold them Mr. Percy?" Jaxon asked.

As Jaxon held onto this special piece of metal he was really in awe that these were Mr. Percy's actual pilot's wings from his service to our country.

"When you wore your pilot's wings you didn't wear any other service medals because if the enemy caught you and knew your ranking it would be bad news," Mr. Percy said. "I actually have 2 pair of pilot's wings... and I would like for you to have a pair, Jaxon."

"No way! Oh no, I can't take your pilot's wings, Mr. Percy," Jaxon said as he handed them back to him.

"Please Jaxon, I want you to have them. The one I am giving you is a backup set in the event I would lose the one I always flew with but as luck had it I never lost them!" Mr. Percy

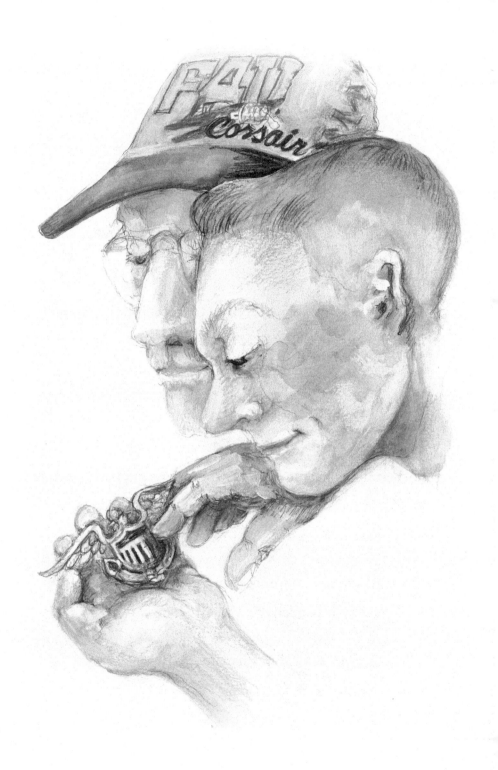

said with a smile. "Now you have a real set of World War II Pilots Wings to remember our trip to Washington, D.C."

With a great big hug you could tell that this meant a lot to both Mr. Percy and Jaxon. Grant looked at Mrs. Percy and smiled. They knew these two would be best buddies from this point forward.

It was getting late and Grant and Jaxon needed to head home to eat dinner with the girls.

"Mr. & Mrs. Percy, we can't thank you enough for the great conversations, history lesson and guidance you have given both of us this afternoon," said Grant. "We'll see you soon! Come on buddy, it's time to let Mr. & Mrs. Percy enjoy their dinner and relax for the evening!" Grant said while giving Jaxon's hair a quick tousle.

"Bye!" said Jaxon as he shut the front door.

CHAPTER TWENTY THREE

That next morning as Grant and Jaxon were heading to McGruder's Mercantile to pick up a few supplies for the day, Jaxon turned down the radio.

"Dad, I want to make something for Mr. Percy to put all of his medals in so they aren't just in a random box," he said with a serious voice. "Those medals are something that he earned and he needs to have something so they are displayed properly."

His dad thought for a few moments and said, "You are exactly right Jaxon! I think we can build something just for Mr. Percy to display his military items proudly!" he said with a smile.

They parked the truck and headed inside.

"I think we have most of the items we need at home in the garage but let's pick up some wood glue, black paint and some disposable brushes."

"Hey there Grant and Jaxon!" said Mac McGruder. "What are you guys working on today?" he said as he was restocking the candy rack.

"We are going to build a display box for Mr. Percy so he can showcase his military medals," Jaxon said. Mr. McGruder looked up at Grant and smiled.

"You guys are always doing something nice for other people. My gift to you is a piece of bubblegum for Jaxon and a handshake for you." He said as he handed Grant the items in a paper sack. "Today you don't owe me a thing." He said with a friendly smile.

"Thank you Mac, and this is exactly why we do business with such a great company!" Grant said as they walked out the door.

Since they had just finished a project and weren't going to start another one until the next day, they decided to head back to the house and work on building the display case in the garage. They weren't exactly sure what they wanted

to build but after some discussion they began to gather supplies they needed.

"Ok Jaxon," said Grant. "Let's grab that 8' board, a box of nails and the bag of things we just got at McGruder's Mercantile."

Jaxon began collecting items while Grant was thinking about what type of a display box to build based on the medals and ribbons he had seen in Mr. Purdy's box.

"Jaxon, will you see if that old picture frame with glass is still over in the corner by the workbench?" asked Grant.

"This one dad?" Jaxon asked as he held up the big frame.

"Yep! That's the one!" Grant said. "Can you bring it over to our work table please!"

After a few quick drawings of what they wanted to make Grant and Jaxon begin measuring and cutting the 8' board and started putting their idea of a display box together. Grant loved working alongside Jaxon. Jaxon was becoming so creative in his thinking and came up with a great idea for making the display box something you could open to get a closer look at items placed inside or perhaps even change things out from time to time.

They worked a good portion of the day to finish up the display case. After dinner they would put the final coat of paint on it. "Come on boys! It's time for dinner!" said Ava.

"Awesome, my favorite!" said Jaxon as they walked into the kitchen.

"I know you love lasagna and after all the hard work you have put in lately I figured I would surprise you!" said his mom. Abbygail must have liked it too because she had it all over her face!

"Bubby, more?" Abbygail asked

"Well, sure I'll have more, Abbygail!" Jaxon said with a gentle tickle under her chin.

After dinner Grant and Jaxon went out to the garage to put one last coat of paint on the display case and then turned the lights off as they went inside. It was going to be a busy day tomorrow and Jaxon needed to get ready for bed.

His parents came in his room to tuck him in and told him how much they loved him. As they were walking out of his room, Jaxon sat up in bed and said, "Mom and dad,

I just wanted to say thank you for everything you do for Abbygail and me. I know we don't say it enough but we both appreciate you."

Jaxon's mom and dad both smiled really big and gave him one last hug. "Jaxon, we really appreciate *you*! We thank our lucky stars everyday that we have someone as thoughtful and caring as you!"

The next day after work they delivered the display case to Mr. Percy. "Mr. Percy, my dad and I built this for you to display your military medals. They deserve to be displayed proudly rather than kept in a box that no one ever sees," Jaxon said.

"With your permission we would like to take your medals and have them placed in the proper order within this display case. We have already talked to the local military frame shop and they would be happy to get this done today so that we can have this back to you by this evening," Grant said with a genuine smile.

"Well, thank you for making this for me and I suppose that would be alright with me if you have them properly displayed. When you bring them back this evening we will find the perfect spot to hang it!" said Mr. Percy

★ ★ ★

"Well, hey there Walt!" said Grant. "Here's the special project I was telling you about the other day. Here's the display case, Mr. Percy's military medals and a few special photos that we would like to add."

"That sounds great Grant! We will get started on this right away and have it ready to be picked up by 3:00 PM." Walt said with a friendly handshake.

CHAPTER TWENTY FOUR

Later that afternoon, at Mr. & Mrs. Percy's house, Grant and Jaxon carried in the display case wrapped in bubble wrap to protect it during the drive.

"Mr. Percy, open your present!" said Jaxon with a giddy smile and laugh.

As Mr. Percy removed the bubble wrap and saw the beautiful display case with his medals and a couple of very special photos from the trip, he couldn't help but tear up.

"I absolutely love this gift and will cherish it forever. I have talked more about my military career in the past few weeks than I have in my lifetime." Mr. Percy wiped his eyes with a handkerchief. "I can't tell you how much it meant to go on the Hero Tour with you two. It truly was a trip to remember. I especially love this photo," he said while pointing to it in the display case, "and will never forget how much you guys mean to Mrs. Percy and me," Mr. Percy said with the most sincere expression on his face. "Thank you!"

Jaxon gave Mr. Percy a big hug. Grant shook his hand followed by a big hug.

"Well," beamed Mrs. Percy, "where are we going to hang this beautiful piece of history?" she said with a big smile. "How about right here next to Mr. Percy's recliner and end table?" she asked.

With teamwork they managed to secure Mr. Percy's display case in the most perfect spot in the house!

"Thank you Mr. Percy for serving our country so proudly and protecting our freedoms that I get to enjoy today," Jaxon said.

Mr. Percy stood up and saluted Jaxon and said, "It wasn't easy but I'm proud to have served."

That evening after dinner Ava noticed that Jaxon had a pencil and paper and was sitting writing something at the kitchen table. "Hey Jax, what are you doing buddy?" his mom asked.

Jaxon finished his sentence and looked up at his mom. "I am doing my summer homework to turn in tomorrow," he said quickly while deep in thought.

"You had homework for summer?" she asked.

"We are supposed to write about something that we did over summer break that forever changed our life for the better," he said in between thoughts.

"Ok, buddy; you only have about 30 minutes until you need to take a shower and get ready for bed." she said.

"Ok, mom," said Jaxon.

CHAPTER TWENTY FIVE

"Jaxon, it's the first day of 5th grade!" his mom said as he walked down the hallway into the kitchen. "Where did this summer go?" she asked. Jaxon gave a smile and rubbed his eyes to wake up a little more.

"Hi bubby!" said his little sister Abbygail as she was excited to see him this morning. Jaxon walked over and gave her a kiss on the head and sat down to have his pancakes.

"Have a great first day of 5th grade, Jaxon... and I'm sure going to miss having you at work today," said his dad as he dropped him off at school.

"Bye, dad! Me, too." said Jaxon.

Jaxon and his buddies had a fun time on the playground and the first person Jaxon went to see was an old friend.

"Hey Carter!" said Jaxon. "I've missed you buddy. How have you been?"

"I've been doing good since my dad got back home from an overseas deployment. He had been been over serving our country for the past 13 months and it hasn't been easy with him being gone." said Carter as he gave Jaxon a fist bump.

"When you go home tonight give your dad a firm handshake and tell him that I said thank you! Oh and I've got something for you buddy!" Jaxon said with a big smile as he reached in his backpack

"You got me a new yo-yo?" asked Carter. "How did you know I wanted one?"

Jaxon just smiled and said, "I overheard you say that yours broke at the end of the school year and I bought you a new red one with lights this summer," said Jaxon.

"Thank you Jaxon buddy!" said Carter.

"Now let's go play four square!" said Jaxon as he grabbed Carter's arm to motion him to come with him to the playground.

Once the school bell rang Jaxon and his classmates headed to their classroom. On the way Mrs. Gentry, the school principal, was saying good morning to everyone as they passed by. Jaxon had loved to have Mrs. Sappington as his 4th grade teacher and now she would be teaching their 5th grade class too!

"Alright, class, who took time to write an essay on your summer break?" Mrs. Sappington said as several hands went into the air. "Please take a moment to pass them to the front of the classroom," said Mrs. Sappington. "I will grade them over the weekend. There will be 3 winning essays and they will be placed outside our classroom on the bulletin board."

Friday afternoon the phone rang. "Hello Mrs. James?" said the voice on the other end of the line.

"Yes, it is. How can I help you?" Ava asked.

"This is Mrs. Sappington, Jaxon's 5th grade teacher. I just wanted to say what a pleasure it is to have Jaxon in my class again this year. He is so thoughtful and students in our school really look up to him," she explained. They talked for a little while longer and then hung up the phone.

★ ★ ★

On Monday morning, the students of Eagle Ridge Elementary School met in the gym for their "Monday Morning Message." Mrs. Gentry made a couple announcements before the students said the Pledge of Allegiance followed by the school song. Then Mrs. Sappington came onto the stage.

"At the end of last year I knew I was going to be teaching 5th grade to my then 4th graders," she said. "I asked them to write an essay about something they did over the summer that impacted them in a positive way. I received twenty essays out of twenty four students. I had the pleasure, along with Mrs. Gentry, to read and choose the top three essays," Mrs. Sappington said as she prepared to read the first essay that stood out to them.

The first essay she read was from Shelby Summers. She had a really good friend that was diagnosed with cancer and together they built hat racks to donate to Clarkson's Cancer Hospital and placed hats on them that anyone could take if they had lost their hair due to treatment. They called this project "Tom T's Hat Rack" and she was extremely proud to give back to her community and make a positive difference in the lives of others. Shelby's mom, dad, Mr. & Mrs. T were there as a surprise.

"I would like to read a portion of the second essay that really stood out to us," said Mrs. Sappington.

"This summer was like no other summer. It was awesome, amazing and memorable. While I thought my very first vacation would be spent with my family our plans changed and I had the opportunity to spend 17+ hours with some of the most incredible true American Heroes."

"My dad was a guardian for Lt. Col. F. A. Percy, a retired World War II pilot and I had the honor to serve as Mr. Percy's junior guardian on a Hero Tour. This very special trip was fast paced, emotional and educational but I learned so much about a wonderful man that I have known since I could walk. Within the past several weeks I have learned so much about his military career and I admire him that much more."

"I learned a lot about our local Eagle City Hero Tour Organization and I wanted to help. I wanted to give back to those that gave so much to our country and what I got in return was far more than I could have ever imagined. I donated my own hard earned money so that two veterans were able to go on this trip. I will do my best to give what I can each year to help other veterans have this opportunity."

"After all, they wrote a blank check to the United States of America for up to and including their life to protect our country and our freedom. This was the least I could do to have a rare opportunity to spend the day with them but most importantly with two men that I love and admire—my dad and Mr. Percy. What I witnessed and experienced while on this once in a lifetime trip will be something I never forget."

"Being able to give back to our community and to donate to such a deserving organization was one of the most rewarding things I have ever done. Next time you are at the store, library or walking on the street and you see the word "veteran", a branch of service on their hat, shirt or jacket or wearing a military uniform I ask that you take a moment to stop, shake their hand and thank them for their service. It will mean more to them than you can ever imagine. It's the least we can do for our veterans. I'm not sure how I was chosen to be on this flight but I can tell you that I am forever grateful."

Mrs. Sappington motioned for Jaxon to come stand next to her and Shelby. and The students and staff—everyone—started clapping and cheering as he made his way onto the stage.

"This young man is the author of this story essay," said Mrs. Sappington. "It is because of his hard work, dedication and commitment to our community that we have chosen Jaxon's essay."

Jaxon was happy – he then noticed that his mom was holding his sister, his dad, Mr. & Mrs. Percy were standing in the back of the gym!

Mrs. Sappington got the gym quieted down and asked, "I want each of you to ask yourself this question every single day. What can you do for someone else today that will impact them in a positive way?"

She turned to Jaxon. "Jaxon, thank you. Your story will not be placed near your classroom as Mrs. Sappington had promised but rather on the big board outside our office for everyone to see as they enter our school along with Shelby's essay," said Mrs. Gentry.

Jaxon gave a quick high five to Mrs. Gentry, Mrs. Sappington and to Shelby before heading over to see his family. "One last thing. I would like to announce that on behalf of the James family they would like to give an additional $1,200.00 so that 4 veterans can go on an upcoming flight!" said Mrs. Sappington with a huge smile and excitement in her voice.

Jaxon was proud, and his family including Mr. & Mrs. Percy were very proud of the young man he was becoming. This summer changed Jaxon. He wasn't the same little boy as when the summer started but rather a more mature young man. There wasn't anything he couldn't do in life with the right attitude and support from his family.

In real life, Lt. Col. Ferrill A. Purdy has not received a Purple Heart Medal for his heroic actions while in combat. We are currently working with our local Congresswoman to submit requested documentation supporting the two incidents where Lt. Col. Ferrill A. Purdy was fired upon by the enemy and survived: once when his plane was hit by enemy fire and he had to land in the ocean, and once when his plane was badly hit, with multiple shrapnel entering his body, yet he was able to coast his plane back to land. There is no guarantee that he will receive a Purple Heart medal; however, with proper documentation our Congresswoman's office will attempt to expedite his case to present to the appropriate federal agency. Our hopes are that Lt. Col. Ferrill A. Purdy will receive a Purple Heart in the coming months.

During the process of writing this book and listening to Lt. Col. Ferrill A. Purdy's military history he often spoke highly of his wing man, Major John H. Tashjian. His name kept running through my head and I wanted to find this young man as he meant an awful lot to Mr. Purdy. After several phone calls and searching on the internet I was able to locate Mr. Tashjian. Together, we would learn that Mr. Tashjian would be attending a symposium in St. Louis, MO at the end of June 2016. Mr. Tashjian made time in his trip to travel to Columbia, MO and on June 26-27, 2016 after 70 years these two Marines were able to reunite in person!

As we gathered documentation needed to submit the Purple Heart medal information we discovered Lt. Col. Ferrill A. Purdy's flight book from World War II. I began researching some of the aircraft he flew and found that one aircraft in particular was unique. The F4U-1 Corsair identified as 17799 was removed from World War II and used in Hollywood as a movie prop. This Corsair has taken part in numerous airshows and flown in a variety of Hollywood productions. Lt. Col. Ferrill A. Purdy flew this plane on June 24, 1944 and again on July 3, 1944.

This F4U-1 Corsair is now a part of the collection at Planes of Fame Air Museum in Chino, California and is currently the oldest airworthy Corsair in the world. They have owned this aircraft since 1966 and have been un-successful in pairing this plane with a pilot until June 15, 2016 when documentation was shown that Lt. Col. Ferrill A. Purdy was one of its pilots during World War II. On June 26, 2016 with proper documentation, we were also able to link Major John H. Tashjian to this plane as well showing that he flew this plane on June 10, 1944. After 50 years they have been able to link this aircraft and now give it proper recognition as a "combat veteran".

www.planesoffame.org

ABOUT THE AUTHOR

After writing my first book, I knew I would like to write a second book but I didn't know what it would be about. After giving it some thought, I was inspired to write about a Veteran. I was looking for a specific character and on June 11, 2013 that young man walked through our business doors. Within a few moments of talking, I knew he would play an important role in this next book.

Over the past 4+ years I have had the opportunity to work with an incredible woman and mentor, Sarah Hill who introduced me to some true American heroes and from that point my life would never be the same. Through technology, we used live streaming and virtual reality tours to take Veterans too sick to physically travel on live trips to see their memorials in Washington, D.C. This allowed me the opportunity to get involved with Central Missouri Honor Flight. Since 2009, Central Missouri Honor Flight has taken 40 flights with 2,500 veterans serving from World War II, Korea and Vietnam to our Nation's Capital to see their memorials.

Lt. Col. Ferrill A. Purdy is a retired Marine Pilot who served two tours in World War II. While Mr. Purdy won't go on an Honor Flight, he allowed me the chance to tell his story to you. It is with great honor and respect that we know the true sacrifices that our veterans gave to protect our country and our freedom. Always remember to thank a veteran as they are the reason you are here today..

ABOUT THE ILLUSTRATOR

A native of Kansas City, Missouri, Peggy A. Guest majored in Fine Art at Christian College, University of Missouri-Columbia, Kansas City Art Institute and Park University. She graduated in 1976, and began working, as an illustrator, for the Department of Defense (Air Force Communications Command) at Richards-Gebaur Air Force Base in Kansas City. She transferred to the Department of the Army and worked for several years at Ft. Leavenworth, Kansas in the Media Support Center. She was promoted to writer/editor for the Army Recruiting Command in Kansas City, Missouri until transferring to USDA'a Crop Insurance Program in 1989, as a graphics/printing supervisor. Peggy and her husband, Joe, started Guest Design Studio in 1992. The studio provides clients with design, murals, fine art painting, sculpture, exhibits, displays and special projects. She was listed in the Who's Who in American Women Artists in 2000. Peggy has painted murals in Fayette, Missouri to promote the town's businesses and is currently working on exhibits at an antique car museum. She is also working on two 32 square foot maps of Fayette, Missouri. She and her husband, Joe, live and work in their studio outside Fayette, Missouri.

Visit her at www.PeggyGuest.com

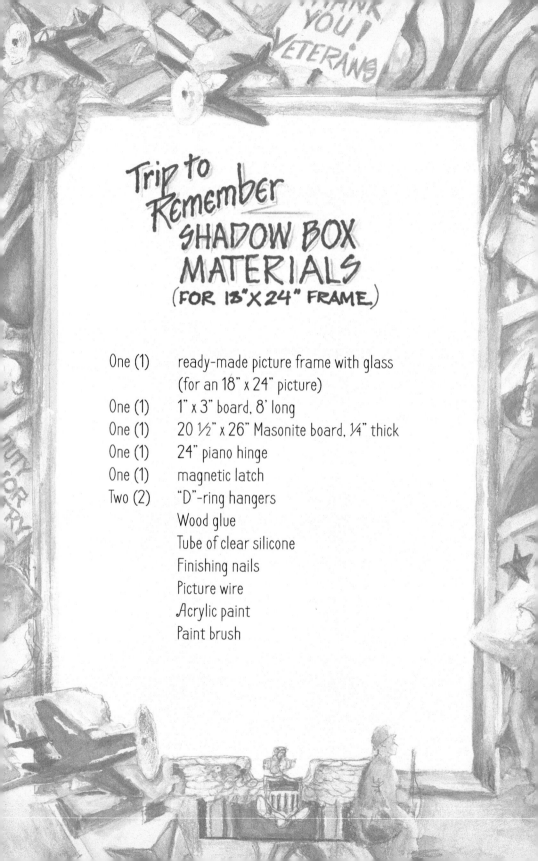

Trip to Remember
SHADOW BOX
MATERIALS
(FOR 18" X 24" FRAME)

One (1)	ready-made picture frame with glass (for an 18" x 24" picture)
One (1)	1" x 3" board, 8' long
One (1)	20 ½" x 26" Masonite board, ¼" thick
One (1)	24" piano hinge
One (1)	magnetic latch
Two (2)	"D"-ring hangers
	Wood glue
	Tube of clear silicone
	Finishing nails
	Picture wire
	Acrylic paint
	Paint brush

DIRECTIONS

① Remove glass from frame and set aside. Paint frame desired color, and let dry.

② Attach one side of piano hinge to edge of long side of frame.

③ Cut 1" x 3" board into four (4) pieces –
two (2) 20 ½" pieces, and two (2) 25-inch pieces. Paint all surfaces and smooth side of the masonite, and let dry.

④ Assemble shadow box. Glue short sides to long sides using half-lap joints. Glue and nail corners.

⑤ Attach magnetic latch and masonite backing to box with glue and finish nails, smooth black side on the inside. Screw other side of piano hinge to box front.

⑥ Turn case and attach D-Rings and wire 8-inches from top of case.

⑦ Clean glass and replace inside frame. Use a small amount of clear silicone around the inside of the frame and glass to create a bead around entire inside of frame to hold the glass in place. Let dry at least 24 hours.

⑧ Mount items inside display box and enjoy!

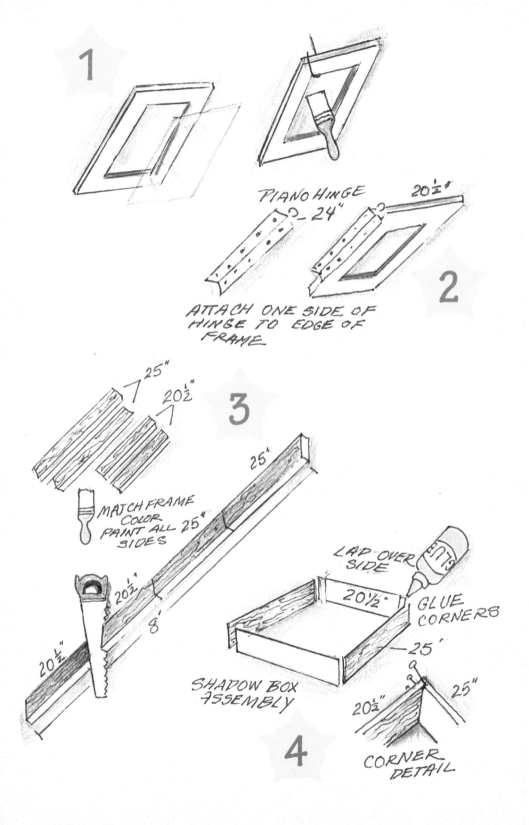

1

2

PIANO HINGE
-24"
20½"

ATTACH ONE SIDE OF
HINGE TO EDGE OF
FRAME

3

25"
20½"

MATCH FRAME
COLOR
PAINT ALL 25"
SIDES

25"

20½"

8'

20½"

LAP-OVER
SIDE

GLUE

20½"

GLUE
CORNERS

—25'

SHADOW BOX
ASSEMBLY

20½"   25"

CORNER
DETAIL

4

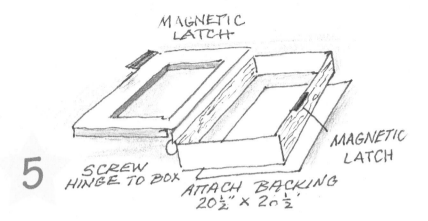

MAGNETIC LATCH

MAGNETIC LATCH

5

SCREW HINGE TO BOX

ATTACH BACKING
$20\frac{1}{2}$" X $20\frac{1}{2}$"

ATTACH "D" RINGS AND WIRE TO BACK

8"

6

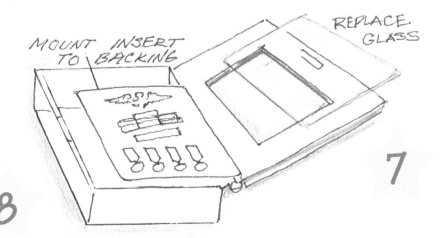

MOUNT INSERT TO BACKING

REPLACE GLASS

7

8

Hopefully this story has inspired you to look through your family's military history. If you happen to find military documents, including medals/ribbons, we encourage you to visit
www.ezrackbuilder.com
to find out the appropriate order or precedence for the military medals/ribbons to be properly displayed.

CPSIA information can be obtained
at www.ICGtesting.com
Printed in the USA
BVOW10*0452261116

468844BV00007B/8/P